# ROBBERS

**CAROL WATSON**

**Illustrated by
STEPHEN CARTWRIGHT**

## CONTENTS

**Series editor: Heather Amery**

Consultant: Eric Maple
Reading Expert: Betty Root
Centre for the Teaching of Reading
University of Reading

CW00950071

# Tom Blood

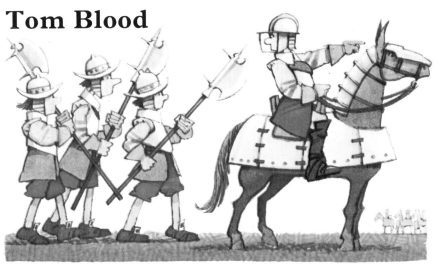

Once there was a brave soldier called Tom Blood. He went away to fight in a war.

When the war ended Tom went home to his wife, but she was not there. The house was empty.

After a long search he found her in London. She was very poor and lived in one tiny room.

"What's happened?" Tom asked. "The King has taken our house and land," said his wife.

Tom was very angry. He walked up and down the little room, scratching his head and thinking.

At last he said, "I have an idea. The King has stolen from me. I shall steal from the King."

Next day when Tom was out walking, he saw a large crowd. It was the King and his courtiers.

The King was going to the Tower. He kept his great crown and all his finest jewels there.

Talbot, the keeper of the Tower, unlocked the gate. Tom watched and then hurried home.

He dressed up as a parson. "Come on," he said to his wife, "we're going to the Tower."

At the Tower were lots of people. They were looking at the jewels. The King spent so much money on clothes and parties he always needed more. So he let people pay to see his jewels.

Tom went to the Tower many times. Soon he made friends with Talbot, the keeper.

One day Tom took Jack, his nephew, and two friends to see the King's crown and jewels.

Talbot led them down the dark steps. Tom whispered to Jack, "Stay here and keep watch."

At the bottom of the steps, Talbot unlocked the big door of the jewel room and went in.

"Now!" said Tom and he threw a cloak over Talbot. Then he hit him on the head with

a mallet. "Quick," Tom shouted to his friends, "grab all the jewels you can carry!"

4

They stuffed jewels
into their pockets. Tom
took the crown and
filled that as well.

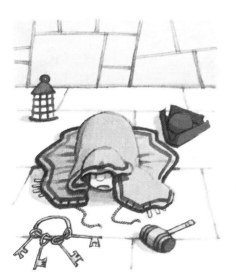

Suddenly Talbot shouted,
"Help! Help!" Jack
called out, "Run, the
guards are coming!"

Three guards rushed
down the stairs and into
the room. They tripped
over Talbot and landed

in a heap on the floor,
shouting and struggling.
Tom slipped out of the
door and up the stairs.

He ran out of the Tower. A guard tried to stop him but Tom quickly knocked him down.

The captain of the guard came round a corner and tripped Tom up. "Got you, rogue," he said.

"Guards!" he shouted. The guards ran up, grabbed Tom and took away the jewels.

Then they marched him to prison and locked him in a dungeon. They tied his wrists with chains.

Soon the guards brought in Jack and Tom's two friends. The jailor brought bread and water.

"What will they do to us?" asked Jack. "You will all hang for this," said the jailor.

Next day, Tom was taken to the Palace. The King sat on his throne looking very grand.

"This man tried to steal your crown and jewels," said the captain of the guard. "He must die."

The King was very angry. He stood up and shouted, "What have you to say, Tom Blood?"

"Sire," said Tom, "you took my house and lands, so I took your crown and jewels."

The King sat down. Then he laughed. "You are a rogue," he said, "but a clever one.

I will pardon you." He gave Tom back his house and land and made him a courtier.

# The Robber Monk

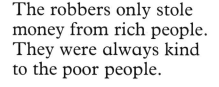

Once there was a band of robbers who lived in a cave. Their leader was called Kurt.

The robbers only stole money from rich people. They were always kind to the poor people.

Each day they hid near the road. Then they leapt out and robbed travellers who came by.

One day a fat merchant rode along with a large box of gold. "Get him, lads," Kurt shouted.

The robbers leapt out to snatch the gold. They did not see the soldiers close by.

"Help! Thieves!" the merchant screamed. The soldiers galloped up to rescue him.

"Grab the leader," one shouted. They jumped off their horses and surrounded Kurt.

The soldiers tried to catch Kurt but he hit them with his stick and ran off.

He ran and ran into the forest. When he stopped to rest, he saw a man walking along the path.

Kurt seized the man. "I'll not harm you if you give me your clothes," he said

Kurt tied the man up. Then, disguised as a smart gentleman, he set off along the road.

The soldiers were searching for him, so he hurried to a large building nearby.

It was a monastery. Kurt knocked on the door. An old monk hobbled out. "Can I help you?" he asked.

"I want to become a monk," Kurt replied. They went inside. The soldiers rode past the door and Kurt was safe.

Kurt became a monk and lived in the monastery for a while. The other monks liked him as he made them laugh.

They told him stories about the monastery. "There are secret doors and tunnels hidden in the walls," they said.

One day Kurt was exploring the monastery when he tripped over the Abbot's cat. He fell against the wall.

Suddenly, a small door opened. "It's a secret tunnel," Kurt thought, and climbed in.

He crawled along the tunnel until he came to some steps. At the top there was a trapdoor.

Kurt pushed it open, and saw he was in a room with a rich lady. She was counting her gold.

The lady was Griselda. She was mean, and never gave money to people who begged at her door.

Kurt went back to the monastery. As he sat in the garden, he saw a robber friend in a tree.

"When are you coming back, Kurt? he asked. "Soon," said Kurt. "I have a plan. Listen."

That night the band of robbers crept silently through the forest to Griselda's house.

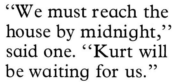

"We must reach the house by midnight," said one. "Kurt will be waiting for us."

The thin robber dressed as a beggar. He knocked on Griselda's door. "Go away!" she shouted.

While the robbers were on their way, Kurt crawled through the tunnel to the trapdoor.

When Griselda went to see the beggar, Kurt climbed into the room where she kept her gold.

He dragged the boxes to the window, and threw them down to the robbers waiting below.

Next day Griselda went to count her gold but the room was empty. "It's gone," she sobbed.

In the monastery the monks searched for Kurt. All they found were his clothes in an empty room.

Kurt jumped down to join the robbers. Then they all ran off to their secret cave.

Back in the cave the robbers had a huge feast. Kurt invited all the poor people.

"Here's gold for you all," he laughed. "Griselda has given it to you at last."

# The Tale of Moll Cutpurse

Once there was a big, clumsy girl called Moll. She had huge hands and feet, and liked playing rough games with boys. One day her mother said, "Moll, you must go to work as a lady's maid."

Moll did not want to be a maid. That night she dressed up as a boy and ran away from home.

The next day Moll was walking in a town. She saw a man stealing from someone's pocket.

"That looks easy," Moll thought. "I'll try it." She did, and she became a clever pickpocket.

"This is better than being a maid" she said, when she counted the gold she had stolen.

One day Moll slipped her hand into a pocket to steal a purse. Her hand was so big it got stuck.

"Help! Thief!" cried the owner. Moll pulled and pulled until out came her hand. She ran away.

She reached her house without being caught. Moll thought up a plan and told her friends.

"My hands are too big to pick pockets," she said, "but I will teach you all my tricks."

The pickpockets gave the money they stole to Moll. She bought a house and they all lived in it.

Soon Moll's house was a hide-out for robbers. They gave her some of the things they stole.

Many people heard about Moll. Rich men who had precious things stolen from their houses went to her to buy their goods back again. They paid her well so Moll grew very rich.

Moll often gave feasts for her robber friends. They ate and drank and

sang funny songs. They told her stories of their adventures and showed her the gold and jewels they had stolen. Moll laughed at them. But she began to think that staying at home all the time was very dull.

One day Moll said to her friends, "I'm bored. It's time I robbed someone again."

That night she dressed up as a highwayman. She crept out of the house and stole a horse.

Then Moll rode off over the fields into the countryside until she came to the highway.

She hid behind a tree. At dawn she heard the sound of horses. A smart carriage came by.

It was Lord and Lady Fogg on their way to town. "What a stroke of luck," thought Moll.

She rode out waving her pistol. "Your money or your life," she shouted at Lord Fogg.

"You'll not have my money," Lord Fogg said. So Moll fired the pistol and shot him in the arm.

His wife screamed and fainted, but Moll grabbed their gold and rode off in a hurry.

Just then, some soldiers rode up. They chased Moll until her horse tripped and fell down.

Moll struggled with the soldiers. She kicked and punched but they won and took her away.

The guards locked Moll up in a dark and gloomy prison to punish her for her wicked ways. Before long, they had caught all her friends and thrown them into the prison too.

# Farmer Will

Each day Will got up at dawn. He took his tools from the shed and went to work on his farm.

Many years ago there was a farmer called Will. He had a wife called Flo, and eighteen children.

Farmer Will was a big, jolly man. He was kind to his family and always helped his neighbours.

Everyone thought Will worked in the fields all day, as he never came home until evening.

They felt sorry for him.
He seemed to work so
hard, yet his crops did
not grow well.

But Will had a secret.
In one of his fields,
hidden behind some
trees, was an old barn.

Each morning Will
worked for an hour. Then
he went to the barn. In
the barn was a cupboard.

It was full of cloaks,
hats, false beards and
wigs. Each day Will put
on a different disguise.

Sometimes Will robbed houses. He stole from his neighbours and even robbed his friends.

Then, making sure no one saw him, he went to the roadside and hid behind a tree. When someone came by, Will jumped out. "Give me your money or I'll kill you," he shouted.

He knew what time they went out, when they came home and where they hid their money.

He put everything in a box in the barn. "Lots of lovely money," he laughed, counting it.

Then he changed out of his disguise, put mud on his boots and went home, looking very tired.

One day Sam Nobbs, the landlord, came to collect the rent. "You owe me two hundred gold pieces, Will," he said.

Flo looked worried. She did not think they had enough money to pay Sam. But Will laughed and counted out the gold.

When the landlord had gone, Will said "I'm late for work."

He kissed Flo goodbye, grabbed his spade and rushed to the fields.

23

He went to the barn and quickly put on a big false beard, a wig and a long red cloak.

Then he hurried to the roadside and waited. Sam Nobbs walked along, whistling happily.

"Hand over your money if you want to stay alive!" Will cried seizing Sam by the throat.

"Take it, but don't kill me!" Sam screamed. He gave Will the bag of gold and ran away.

That evening, when Will went home, Sam Nobbs was there telling Flo what had happened.

"The robber has black hair, a big, bushy beard and a long, red cloak," Sam said. "So beware!"

24

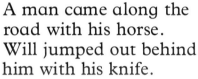

The next day Will wore something quite different when he went off to rob someone.

A man came along the road with his horse. Will jumped out behind him with his knife.

The man was very big and strong. "Got you, thief!" he cried, and hit Will so hard that he knocked him out.

Then he tied Will's hands and feet, and slung him over his horse. He took Will to the sheriff in town.

Two soldiers marched Will to the market place and locked him in the stocks.

"They've caught the robber," a woman cried. "Come and see the wicked villain."

"Take that, you beast!" she screamed, and she threw a big cabbage at Will's head.

Everyone came to stare at Will and they pelted him with rotten fruit and bad eggs.

Flo was at the market doing her shopping. She went to see what all the noise was about.

It hit Will's head so hard, it knocked off his wig. And then his beard fell off too.

Flo could not believe
her eyes. "It's my Will,"
she cried, and she
fainted with shock.

Everyone was surprised
that kind, hardworking
Will turned out to be
the wicked robber.

Next day, the judge
said to Will, "You will
go to prison for the
rest of your life."

"Oh no," cried Flo.
"Please Sir, all the
children and I will work
to pay back the money."

"Very well," said the
judge. "But Will must
go to prison for five
years." The soldiers
led Will away.

# The Snake Charmer

Long ago in India,
there lived a snake
charmer called Raj. His
wife was called Akba.

They had a deadly snake
which they kept in a
pot. No one had ever
charmed such a snake.

When Raj played a tune
on his pipe, the snake
swayed from side to side
in time to the music.

One day Raj said,
"Today I'll try my luck
in the market place."
So off he went.

At the market Raj sat
down on a rug, took the
lid off the pot and
began to play a tune.

"Look at this snake,"
a man called out. "Come
and see." Soon lots
of people came to look.

They paid Raj money to see him charm the snake. At the end of the day Raj had a pile of gold.

Four robbers watched Raj. "Look at all that money," they whispered. "Let's steal it."

The robbers followed Raj home. They watched as Akba counted the gold into a large pot.

That night they tried to break into the house. One robber stubbed his toe. "Ow!" he yelled.

The noise woke up Akba. "There's someone outside, Raj," she said. "It's only a dog," he replied. "Go to sleep."

"Tomorrow I'll put our gold up in the store room," Akba said. "It will be much safer at the top of the house."

"I can see the pot," he whispered. He tried to climb in, but the window was too small.

The next evening Akba took the pot of gold upstairs. "Take the snake," said Raj, "that's precious too."

That night the robbers came back. The smallest robber climbed up the others so that he could look in the window.

He pushed and squeezed until he was half into the room. He was just able to reach the pot.

"I've got it," he said. The robbers carefully passed the pot down to the ground.

"Let's take it back to our den," said the small robber. They ran off home in the dark.

"Now we are rich," the small robber said, and he took the lid off the pot. Then he screamed and fell down dead.

"It's the poisonous snake," the robbers gasped. They ran away in fright and were never seen again.

The next morning Raj wanted to go to the market again. Akba went upstairs to fetch down the snake.

"One of the pots has gone," she cried. She took the lid off the other pot. The gold was still there.

First published in 1981 by
Usborne Publishing Ltd,
20 Garrick Street,
London WC2 9BJ, England.

"The robbers took the wrong pot," laughed Raj. "They must have had a nasty shock."

He sat down, played a tune on his pipe and, in no time at all, the snake came slithering home.

Printed in Belgium by CASTERMAN S.A.